Goes To The Farm

PUFFIN BOOKS

Dear Parents

This story depicts many typical farm activities. The realism of the photographs will help young children discover life on a farm along with Barney, Baby Bop and BJ. Young children will enjoy making animal sounds as they read about the hard work, as well as the fun, that happens on a farm.

We consider books to be lifelong gifts that develop and enhance the love of reading. We hope you enjoy reading along with Barney and Baby Bop!

Mary Ann Dudko, Ph.D.
Margie Larsen, M.Ed.
Early Childhood Educational Specialists

Art Director: Tricia Legault
Designer: Joseph Hernandez

PUFFIN BOOKS

Published by the Penguin Group under licence from Lyons Partnership, L.P.
Penguin Books Ltd, 27 Wrights Lane, London W8 5TZ, England
Penguin Putnam Inc., 375 Hudson Street, New York, New York 10014, USA
Penguin Books Australia Ltd, Ringwood, Victoria, Australia
Penguin Books Canada Ltd, 10 Alcorn Avenue, Toronto, Ontario, Canada M4V 3B2
Penguin Books (NZ) Ltd, 182–190 Wairau Road, Auckland 10, New Zealand

Penguin Books Ltd, Registered Offices: Harmondsworth, Middlesex, England

First published in the USA by Barney™ Publishing, a division of Lyons Partnership, L.P. 1998
Published in Puffin Books 1998
10 9 8 7 6 5 4 3 2 1

Made and printed in Great Britain by Saxon Profile Press

British Library Cataloguing in Publication Data
A CIP catalogue record for this book is available from the British Library

ISBN 0-140-56448-9

Goes To The Farm

Written by Mark S. Bernthal • Photography by Dennis Full

It was a beautiful morning on the farm! The sun was rising like a big yellow ball and the cockerel was crowing, "Cock-a-doodle-dooooo!"

Barney jumped for joy shouting, "Boy, oh boy! Another day of fun on the farm!"

"I like to play on the farm," said Baby Bop.

"But we have to work today, Sissy," reminded BJ.

"That's right," said Barney. "Farmers start their day early because they always have lots of jobs to do. Let's go to the barn where some of the animals live."

BJ fed fresh hay to Agnes the horse. "Here's your breakfast," BJ said, as Agnes nibbled away happily.

Barney finished milking Bernice the cow, who *mooooed* contentedly.

"Wheeeee!" shouted Baby Bop, as she jumped up and down in the soft haystack.

After feeding Agnes, BJ collected eggs that the chickens had laid. “Aye yie yie! Look at all these eggs!” said BJ.

Baby Bop strutted around making a noise like a chicken – “Cluck, cluck, cluck, cluck!”

Barney got ready to drive the big tractor to the field. “Vroooom vroooom,” said Baby Bop.

Barney and BJ picked sweetcorn in the afternoon sun. “Whew! It’s hot!” sighed BJ, wiping his brow.

Near by, Baby Bop popped her head out of the tall rows of sweetcorn and giggled, “Peek-a-boo, Mr Scarecrow!”

Next, Barney and BJ herded the cows out to the pasture where they could eat a delicious lunch of green grass.

Baby Bop marched ahead ringing a cowbell. “Look at me! I’m leading a cow parade!” she shouted happily.

But the jobs still weren't finished! Barney and BJ picked lots of vegetables from the garden. They filled their baskets with red tomatoes, orange carrots, green beans, and one of Barney's favourite vegetables – purple aubergine!

Baby Bop watched from near by. "This watermelon makes a good seat!" she giggled.

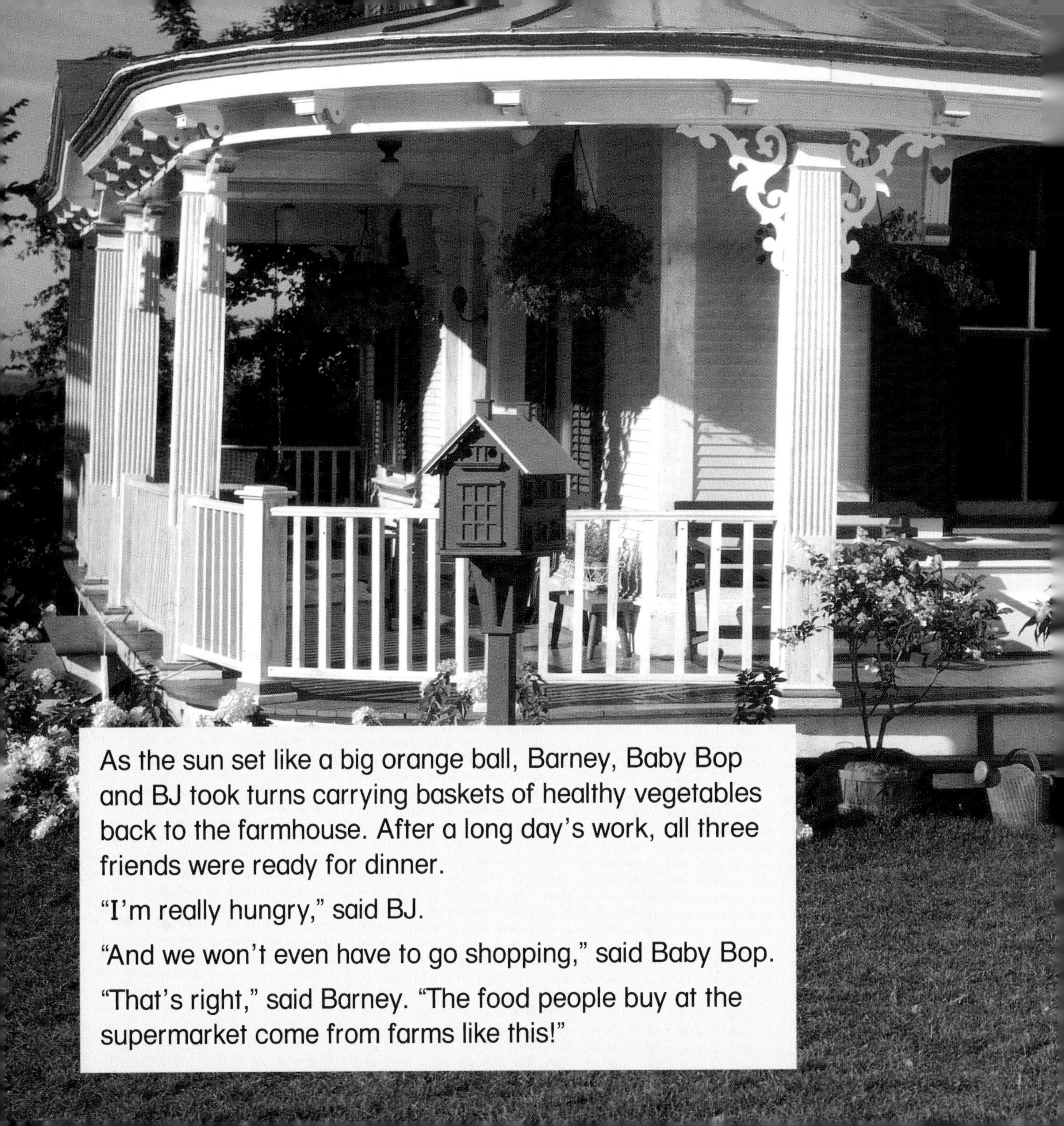

As the sun set like a big orange ball, Barney, Baby Bop and BJ took turns carrying baskets of healthy vegetables back to the farmhouse. After a long day's work, all three friends were ready for dinner.

"I'm really hungry," said BJ.

"And we won't even have to go shopping," said Baby Bop.

"That's right," said Barney. "The food people buy at the supermarket come from farms like this!"

After dinner, Baby Bop fell fast asleep.
"Aye yie yie, Barney! How can Sissy be so tired?" wondered BJ.
"She played as hard as we worked," said Barney with a chuckle.